Do not touch this journal!

EZRA

REBEL JOURNAL
BY EZRA BRIDGER

WARNING
Read one word and
I will slingshot you
into hyperspace!!

studio fun **BOOKS**

White Plains, New York • Montréal, Québec • Bath, United Kingdom

```
TUNED FREQUENCY: 8577.3
SIGNAL CHECK: clear

TUNED FREQUENCY: 8321.0
SIGNAL CHECK: clear

TUNED FREQUENCY: 7911.9¹
SIGNAL CHECK: clear
```

DAY 1

Look what I found in the dust underneath the comm panel — an official communications logbook. The LothalNet techs must have recorded some pretty boring stuff in here — before they shut this tower down, at least. Looks like they didn't get very far.

This logbook could be good for sketching in.

Or for writing in. Like a journal.

Problem: I'm no good at writing.

Ezra, you're ALREADY WRITING.

DOWN WITH THE EMPIRE

So why not, right?

Who else do I have to talk to out here?

I, Ezra Bridger, being of stout heart and keen mind,

This is a stupid idea. JUST FORGET IT.

DAY 7

Got bored enough to pick this thing up again. I mean, why not write a journal? When I'm famous this will be worth big money.

BORED

Trooper=LOSER

So yeah, okay. Here's me! Ezra Bridger.

Learn this face! It'll be on wanted posters soon—"Lothal's untraceable bandit"!

After that, the next place you'll see my face is in the history holos.

"Ezra Bridger: Born on Lothal during the first year of the Empire, now known across the galaxy until the end of time."

I'm not going to talk about the past in this journal. But one of these days I'm going to settle some old scores:

Slyyth, a Capital City fence who recruits orphans to do his dirty work. The Ruurian tried to teach me a little about pickpocketing, but I didn't need the lessons.

And then there are the people who claimed to be friends of my parents. SOME friends.

They know what they did.

You want my advice?

NEVER TRUST ANYBODY

DAY 8

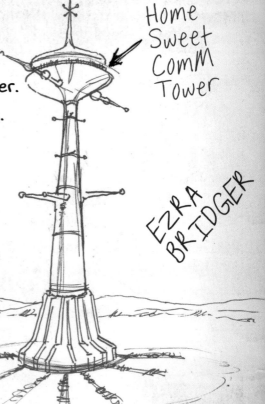

Home sweet comm tower.
Yeah, I live on my own.
But I'm almost
fourteen.

And check out this
PRIME headquarters!

Home
Sweet
Comm
Tower

EZRA
BRIDGER

WAS:
  LothalNet comm
  tower E-272,
  Grid Q6,
  Western Zone

NOW: FORT EZRA!

Hasn't been used for years, not
since the Empire seized the
  western agrizone. Nobody comes
out to check on it either.

Have a tour!

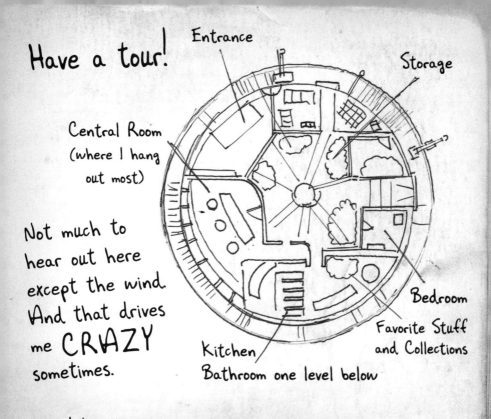

Entrance

Storage

Central Room
(where I hang
out most)

Not much to
hear out here
except the wind.
And that drives
me CRAZY
sometimes.

Bedroom

Favorite Stuff
and Collections

Kitchen
Bathroom one level below

I like to sit up top and look out in every direction.
Especially when the moons are out.

DAY 12

Living on your own is GREAT!

Nobody around to bother you, or tell you what to do.

But there's a downside:
  Nobody GIVES YOU stuff.
  You've got to TAKE IT.

Here are the 3 best things about being a loner:

1. You make your own rules. I sleep whenever I want, wear whatever I want, and go wherever I want.

2. You get your own space. I mean, have you seen Fort Ezra?

3. You grow up. I've learned a lot more on my own than I ever would have in some school somewhere.

For Example...

Everybody for themselves

That's how life works, but nobody ever comes out and says it to your face, they just make you discover it on your own. So don't get disappointed if you're hearing it for the first time. The thing is, once you realize it, nobody can ever let you down again.

DAY 14

LIFE ON LOTHAL.

It's not a bad looking planet. Mountains, grasslands, you know. Lots of farms.

Found this in a travel magazine.

Quiet.

Then the Empire expanded into the Outer Rim. The strip mining made everything smelly and ugly. Farmers who lost their land didn't even get paid, they just got evicted

The rich got richer. Everybody else got desperate, or **mysteriously disappeared.**

I wouldn't mind Lothal being the "gateway to the Outer Rim" if it meant the Empire would stay out in orbit.

But NO, they had to come down and steal our goods too.

Here's a typical farm.

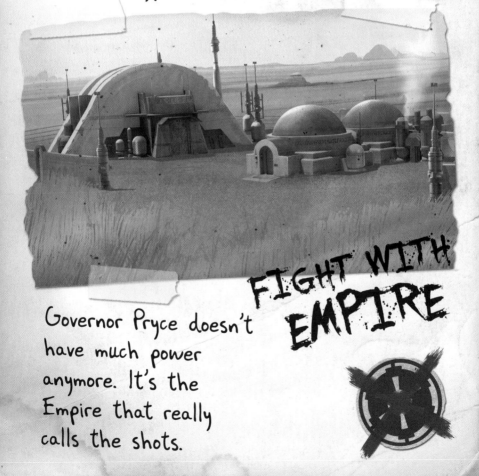

Governor Pryce doesn't have much power anymore. It's the Empire that really calls the shots.

FIGHT WITH EMPIRE

DAY 17   Capital City: THE INSIDER'S GUIDE

This city only has two kinds of people: the rich and everybody else. But you can make it your own, as long as you listen to me.

Guard these secrets with your LIFE!

In the wealthy districts, restaurants throw out tons of food every night. It's good eating the next morning, if the Loth-rats don't get to it first.

Capital City has a huge network of underground tunnels. Good place to make a getaway, but watch out for the creatures down there.

THEY BITE.

From a flier some creature gave me.

BISTRO DE LOTHAL

MEAL OF THE DAY
Four Courses — 125 Credits

Crystal Mushroom Soup

Sautéed Spring Greens of Five Planets

Groat Chop with fresh
Candleberry Reduction Sauce

Soufflé a la Lothal with
Jogan Fruit Drizzle

DAY 18

Always stay alert.

Want to see where I run most of my scams?
Yeah I knew you did.

What, it's not like I have a job in the factories or something. How did you think I made a living?

This is the market district, and here's who I can trust.

These guys have my back. They pretend they don't see me when I'm hiding underneath their tables, and they'll give me food sometimes if they owe me a favor.

The stalls in this row sell fruit, weavings, FRUIT, rebuilt electronics, FRUIT—why is there SO MUCH FRUIT?

Leadership Zone

Spaceport Landings –
Cargo

Spaceport Landings –
Passengers

Trade Bazaar

Spaceport cargo landings. Here's where the big shipments of goods come in. Millions of tons move through here every week. Who's going to notice if a teeny tiny bit of it goes missing?

Hotel District

Spaceport passenger landings. Here's where your marks arrive. They'll be looking for somebody to guide them around the city, and they'll pay you for that. That's when you get a close-up look at anything valuable they're carrying.

This is why I live alone.

EMPIRE MONOSHUTTLE
CAPITAL CITY

Easy • Fast • Safe Transport
No. 1 in the Galaxy! Serving more than 1,500 cities

REMEMBER:

Pay in advance

Single trip	4 credits	
DayPass	10 credits	
Transfers	free	

No weapons allowed.

No selling or soliciting allowed.

Keep all body parts and belongings INSIDE the windows.

Boisterous or annoying behavior will result in prison.

Language insulting to the Emperor or the Empire will result in prison.

Painting or defacing the shuttle will result in prison.

All shuttles are monitored continuously.

Weekly and monthly passes available.

No creatures over 8 feet tall allowed.

No creatures under 2 feet tall allowed.

No creatures with 6 or more arms or legs allowed.

Enjoy the ride!

Then there are Commandant Aresko and Taskmaster Grint, Empire enforcers in Capital City. These guys I definitely CAN'T trust. But I can scam 'em all day long.

NAME: Cumberlayne Aresko
RANK: Imperial Commandant
CODE CYLINDER: LRC-01   HEIGHT: 1.86m
WEIGHT: 80kg
AUTHORIZED TO ACCESS: All Lothal transmissions, recordings, and data archives
AUTHORIZED TO COMMAND: Imperial stormtroopers, all Lothal municipal officials and police forces

I stole his access pass!

Aresko is full of himself. He's hoping for a promotion he's never going to get.

Grint is a big dumb brute who does everything Aresko says.

BUCKETHEADS

How to get around Capital City:

UP AND OVER: if you need to get from one place to another, use the rooftops!

DOWN AND UNDER: same thing, but in the sewers and drainage ditches!

Most of the time you can go wherever you want. TRUST ME, people don't notice anything if it isn't right in front of their faces.

DAY 22

The Empire moves goods through the market district all the time, and that's where somebody like me can come out ahead. Pickpocket an officer. Whistle while I walk off with a crate of Imperial property under my arm.

This is Ferpil.

But stealing stuff from the Empire doesn't do you much good unless you can sell it. Luckily I've got a link to the black market in Ferpil Wallaway. He's a Xexto with his own pawnshop, and he buys almost everything from me to resell to the Broken Horn syndicate.

I win twice — I get paid, and I don't have to deal with Cikatro Vizago. He's the boss of Broken Horn, and from the stories I've heard I hope I never meet him.

That's Vizago.

UGLY!

TODAY'S HAUL

Small crate, magnetically sealed
(had to bash it open with a rock)

CONTENTS: A case of expensive Tynnan mineral water. All the bottles were broken because I bashed the crate open with a rock.

Medium crate, electronic lock
(bypassed with droid arm)

CONTENTS: Power cells. Ferpil offered five credits. I talked him up to eight. Still, what can you buy with eight measly credits?

Large crate, NOT locked

CONTENTS: Inner-layer jumpsuits for TIE pilots. Tried to sell them to Ferpil but he said nobody wants the Empire's underwear.

SO BORED

DAY 28

So I guess I can't avoid talking about the Empire, much as I'd like to. I mean, look at this. If you live on Lothal you can't help but look at this stuff, all day long. It's everywhere.

It's all brainwashing, but anybody who'd listen to this mucus-rot doesn't have a brain to begin with. The "glory of Imperial service" — give me a break. They want suckers to enlist of their own FREE WILL!

NEVER
NEVER JOIN
NEVER
THE IMPERIAL ARMY

EZRA

DOWN WITH THE EMPIRE

Don't get me started on the new Imperial Academy they opened up here on Lothal. Kids just about my age, signing up to become pilots, officers, and stormtroopers.

REBELS RULE

I get mad when people on Lothal give the Empire what they want without putting up a fight. I get even madder when they join the enemy on purpose.

I'm always coming up with better names for stormtroopers:

BUCKETBRAINS

TARGET PRACTICE

Plasteel pigs

The Emperor's Snowmen

Stifftrooperts

Stormbloopers

DAY 37

SO bored. Bored bored bored.

It's raining. No point in going into the city on days like this. People keep a closer watch on their stuff when they're afraid it might get wet.

I made up a game using bolts and screws but I'm not sure if it's any good. Here's how you play:

Toss a screw at a circle. If it makes it in, you have to toss a bolt in the same circle before you can keep going.

Draw six circles in the dirt.

Only one bolt and one screw per circle. If you get more in a circle by accident you have to clear that one and do it over.

Game ends when you fill all six circles.

I've been watching these Loth-cats that nest in the tall grass on the tower's south side.

A flight of edgehawks was swooping down on them, trying to grab the weakest animals and make them their dinner. I finally got fed up with it, and chased the birds away with my slingshot.

I'M HUNGRY. AGAIN.

STILL BORED. Rain has been pounding on the metal roof for over a week.

Been trying to decide how I want to organize my collection of helmets. I got these from storm-troopers I defeated in battle! Or at least I hope it looks that way, if anyone ever comes snooping around. Truth is, I snatched most of these from off-duty bucketbrains who weren't keeping a close eye on their buckets.

And here's my jump speeder, which hasn't been working right since I cleaned the repulsorlift coil. Aren't you supposed to clean it? The manual is useless.

HELMETS_

side

GOTTA GET ONE OF THESE

TRANSPORT DRIVER HELMET (STEALTH)

Issued to operators of Imperial Troop Transports and other ground vehicles. Low sensor profile.

front

SPECIAL ADJUTANT'S HELMET

CLASSIFIED

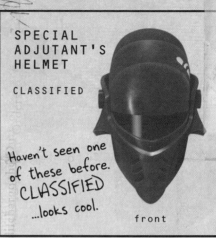

Haven't seen one of these before. CLASSIFIED ...looks cool.

front

CADET HELMET (TACTICAL)

Issued to Imperial Academy cadets. Features integrated telemetry display.

front

TRANSPORT PILOT HELMET (STANDARD)

Issued to operators of Imperial Troop Transports and other ground vehicles. Lightweight.

side

back

CADET HELMET (COMMAND)

Issued to Imperial Academy squad leaders. Features voice amplification.

front

side

back

HELMETS_

STORMTROOPER HELMET

front

side

Issued to regular-duty Imperial stormtroopers. Features integrated commlink.

AT-DP PILOT HELMET

Issued to operators of AT-DPs and other assault vehicles. Features targeting rangefinder.

front

side

TIE PILOT HELMET

Issued to pilots of Imperial TIE fighters. Features integrated atmosphere supply.

front

side

ISB (IMPERIAL SECURITY BUREAU) AGENT HELMET

side

front

Worn by Imperial commanders in battle.

CADET HELMET (STANDARD)

Issued to Imperial Academy cadets. Features retractable face mask.

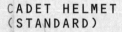

front

side

Thinking about a custom paint job—
flame yellow and fire red.

Now I just need to steal some paints.

Because this is a comm tower I was
wondering if I could pick up Imperial military
transmissions. Instead all I can hear are the
propaganda broadcasts from Alton Kastle,
"Voice of the Empire." Like that's going to
cheer me up.

DAY 57

Pickpocketing tips? Yeah, I'll share a few.

Consider this a peek into the old Ezra magic.
These tips will also help you avoid getting
pickpocketed yourself! You can thank me later.

FIRST THING TO KNOW:

You need to touch your mark in order
to lift their stuff, so disguise
the touch as an innocent bump
or shove. "Sorry sir, didn't see you
there!" They'll yell at you, but by
then you've already got their goods.

SECOND THING:

Don't look like a pickpocket! Look
like a tourist, or a lost kid. The
kind of person you'd NEVER suspect.

THIRD THING:

If you're not sure where a mark keeps his
credits, yell "I'VE BEEN ROBBED!" Everybody
within earshot will pat their pockets, making sure
their money's still there. THAT pocket is your target.

Today I spent all afternoon working the Imperial pavilion. Here's my haul:

- Level 9 COMPNOR ID card.
    Ferpil will buy this.

- Bunch of credits. I'm keeping these.

- Mini holoprojector that plays propaganda vids. Strip it for parts.

- FIRE RUBY.
    Could be worth a fortune, but probably fake.

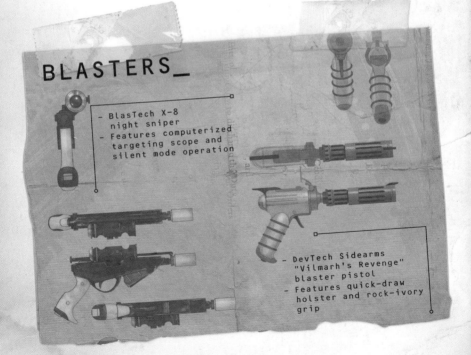

BLASTERS_

- BlasTech X-8 night sniper
- Features computerized targeting scope and silent mode operation

- DevTech Sidearms "Vilmarh's Revenge" blaster pistol
- Features quick-draw holster and rock-ivory grip

Today I spent all afternoon working the Imperial pavilion. Here's my haul:

BLASTERS_

- Concordian Crescent Technologies WESTAR-35 blaster pistol
- Features stun setting and sealed, low-maintenance construction

A

- Merr-Sonn 773 Firepuncher
- Features ablative coating and wide-beam "burning" mode

B

STORMTROOPER BLASTER

- BlasTech DL-18
- Features long barrel and overconcentrated beam for extra firepower

- BlasTech E-11 blaster rifle
- Features extendable stock and fully automatic fire setting

FIGHT THE EMPIRE

DAY 60

So I rigged the tower with booby traps.
CHECK IT OUT!

Loose deckplates – step on the
wrong end and they'll flip up
and hit you in the face.

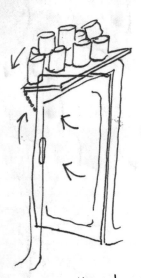

SEE THIS
TARP?

If you push this door open
all the way, you'll pull this
wire. And then these empty
fuel cans will crash down
on your head.

Jump over it. If you try
to stand on it you'll fall
all the way down to the
maintenance sublevel.

FIGHT WITH EMPIRE

I keep running into this girl
in town, Moreena Krai. She's
cool. Haven't told her much
about myself yet.

But I'd probably scare
her off if I did.

DAY 66

PRANKS. Yes, the old Ezra magic comes in handy here too. The same skills that help you steal from the Imperials are also good for exposing them as idiots.

My #3 Prank: Steal an officer's commlink, dip it in grease, and return it to the same guy's pocket. When he puts it up to his face to talk he'll leave a big smear behind!

My #2 Prank: Get a cheap piece of recording circuitry and make it repeat "THE EMPEROR KISSES HUTTS" at full volume. Then hide it in an alleyway. The Imperials will go crazy looking for it, and you can run some other scam while they're busy.

MY #1 PRANK: Shove a stinkfruit under the seat of an Imperial speeder bike. Once the repulsorlift engine heats up, the stench will be so bad the Empire will have to air out the entire garrison.

If someone catches you while you're setting up a prank, don't panic! Just say you're lost, or you're making a delivery, and no sir, you have no idea how that stinkfruit got there, sir.

Tell them what they want to hear and they'll believe it. I'm really good at this stuff. Sometimes it's like I can read people's minds. Crazy, huh?

CAPITAL CITY
Crime Log, day 179843

■ 7:32 a.m.
Wallet snatching, Monoshuttle Brown Line, Station 34. Valued at 125 credits. No suspect. Case no. 23-456-12.

■ 7:45 a.m.
Hit and Run accident, Trade Zone A, potential criminal intent. Perpetrator on silver Jump Speeder, no unusual marks, approx. 3 years old. Failed attempt to steal purse; fled scene. Case no. 23-458-74.

■ 9:18 a.m.
Aggravated theft and defacement of Empire officer commlink, Trade Bazaar. Commlink secretly returned covered in slimy brown grease, causing stains to officer's hands, clothes and face. Suspect a boy, roughly 16-19 years old, riding unlicensed Jumpspeeder. Case no. 23-513-92

DAY 70
SO HUNGRY!

My last scam didn't go so well. Got collared by Taskmaster Grint, but don't worry, I didn't let him get a good look at my face.

Instead I wriggled out of my coat and ran. I left Grint holding an empty coat with a dumb look on his face, but that was a really nice coat.

So I didn't score ANYTHING, and now I have nothing to sell to Ferpil. And NOTHING I can use to barter for food.

Just once I'd like to pull in a dream haul, the kind of score that would set me up for life. A case of nova crystals, maybe. Or a crate of blaster rifles. Hey, if I keep doing what I'm doing it's bound to happen sometime, right?

MY LATEST WISH LIST

Vacuum-sealed, reheatable meals, imported from Chandrila. You can store these forever because they never spoil. And they look DELICIOUS.

DURABLE MATERIAL FOR LONG TERM STORAGE

FOOD POUCHES FLAVORS OF CHANDRILLA SPICY OR MILD

SILK WEAVE DUSK CAMOUFLAGE

Silk weave dusk cape. I could use this to camouflage myself at night. During the day I'd look stylish.

Frontier armor. This stuff is lightweight and flexible from what I've read. Supposedly it can stop a blaster bolt.

DAY 89

I built a training course to practice jumping and climbing! It's all inside the tower!

Ladder I can tip in different directions

Platforms leading to upper level

Swinging rope

Pole for sliding down

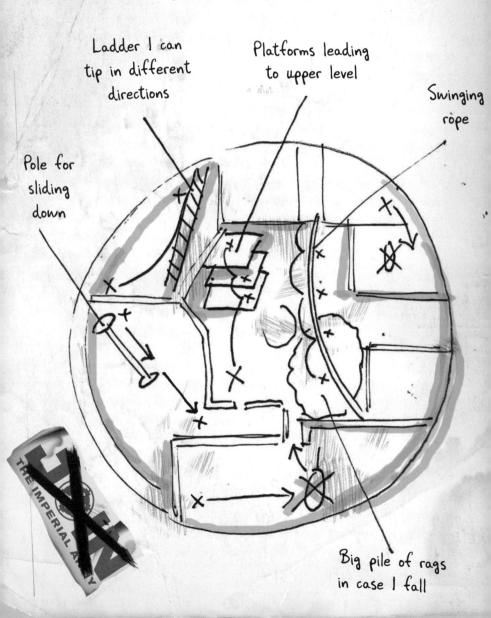

Big pile of rags in case I fall

DAY 93

NO ONE can catch me.

I haven't been using the course much. Feeling pretty down. I had this idea to tame one of the Loth-cats outside, maybe even give it to Moreena as a pet.

EZRA BRIDGER

I fed him. He seemed to like me. But when I set him back down he ran for the door and disappeared into the grass.

I guess I can't blame him.

I drag EVERYBODY down.

DAY 114

I got a job! Ferpil Wallaway hired me to sell tickets at the spaceport. Tickets for what? For Gladiator Night, laser brain! You can't miss the posters, not if I have anything to say about it. For every poster the Empire rips down I stick up two more. I'm earning credits for that too.

TOTAL INSANITY GUARANTEED!

GLADIATOR BATTLE SUPREME

7 BOUTS

NO RULES! NO FEAR! NO STOPPING!

FEATURING
14 WORLD-CLASS BATTLERS
FROM 9 PLANETS
MONAD OUTPOST
THURSDAY 7 P.M.
BE THERE OR BE A SNIVELING WEAKLING

TICKET REQUIRED: 25 CREDITS IN ADVANCE, 35 DAY OF BATTLE

Somebody is turning the old Monad Outpost into an arena. It's about 20 kilometers outside of Capital City. It used to be a place for mining and spaceport operations but now it's empty and abandoned. Except for in a couple days, when it'll be rocking!

It's all totally illegal, which is why they need somebody like me who knows how to sell tickets on the down-low.

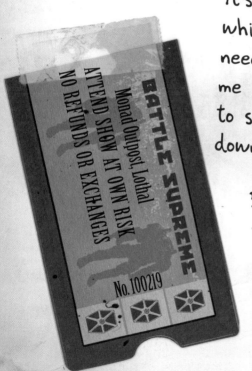

BATTLE SUPREME

Monad Outpost, Lothal

ATTEND SHOW AT OWN RISK
NO REFUNDS OR EXCHANGES

No.100219

Even if I don't get to see the fight, at least I can snatch a few prizes from the pockets of rich suckers.

I am awesome.

Some[...] [...]turning the old
[...]t into an arena.
[...] kilometers outside
[...]. It used to be a
[...] and spaceport
[...]ow it's empty and
[...]pt for in a couple
[...]e rocking!

It's all totally illegal,
which is why they
need somebody like
me who knows how
to sell tickets on the
down-low.

Even if I don't get to
see the fight, at least
I can snatch a few
prizes from the pock-
ets of rich suckers.

I am awesome.

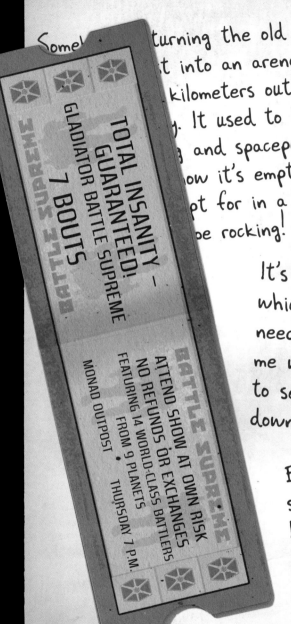

BATTLE SUPREME

TOTAL INSANITY –
GUARANTEED!
GLADIATOR BATTLE SUPREME
7 BOUTS

BATTLE SUPREME

ATTEND SHOW AT OWN RISK
NO REFUNDS OR EXCHANGES
FEATURING 14 WORLD-CLASS BATTLERS
FROM 9 PLANETS
MONAD OUTPOST • THURSDAY 7 P.M.

REBELS RULE

DAY 116

That. Was. Unbelievable.

So I was selling tickets for the fight,
you know, like I said. And then a bounty
hunter came to Lothal. Bossk. He's a
Trandoshan, carries a mortar gun, flies a
YV-series freighter...

Bossk's Freighter, the Hound's Tooth

Why am I writing this down? You can read it all on his ID card, which I swiped!

NAME: Bossk   SPECIES: Trandoshan
HEIGHT: 1.9m   WEIGHT: 113kg
AUTHORIZED TO CARRY: Relby-v10 mortar gun
AUTHORIZED TO PILOT:
CEC YV-series light freighter *Hound's Tooth*

Licensed by the Imperial Office of
Criminal Investigation and the
Bounty Hunters Guild

ALL ACCESS

BOSSK

Serves him right for calling me Shorty.

TRANDOSHANS: Tall. Scaly. Hiss a lot. Have big claws and can't hold on to anything without scratching it. I don't know if this stuff is true for all Trandoshans though. Bossk is kind of the first one I've ever met.

DAY 119

Turns out Bossk needed me, and why not? I know Lothal better than anybody.

He was tracking a bounty and I guess there was a rotten Imperial officer mixed up in it too. Me and Bossk made a pretty good team. It turns out Bossk is pretty well known in the Galaxy. And we made it to Gladiator Night!

Monad Outpost

In a gladiator fight they let you use big weapons, like axes. I'm not as strong as these guys but I'm pretty fast and smart. I seem to have really quick reflexes when it comes to fighting. Or at least when it comes to not getting hit. I might do okay.

These guys are ready for battle.

NEXT DAY

So maybe we didn't make
such a good team after
all. Bossk left the planet
and it looks like he's not coming back.

It's finally sinking in that Ferpil
Wallaway is gone too.

And before that crazy stuff even happened,

Moreena told me how she's moving to

Alderaan to live with her grandmother,

thanks to the Empire condemning her farm.

Last night when I was still riding high
I thought MAYBE I could train to be a
bounty hunter, maybe learn a thing or two
from Bossk. Might as well forget it now.

Everybody leaves.
Everybody ALWAYS leaves.

ALWAYS
ALONE.

BUT WAIT – then this happened! A TIE fighter and a freighter were shooting it out right above my head. And the TIE plowed into the field next to the comm tower.

People fighting the Empire and winning? This is the kind of stuff that never happens on Lothal.

Always stay ALERT

Turned out the pilot was okay, but too bad the crash didn't knock any of the jerkiness out of him.

I stole all the best bits from the wreckage, and didn't feel bad at all. And then when the slimeball fired the TIE's cannons at me? I slingshotted a stun-ball, right into his head.

Here's something else I snatched. Looks like classified info. The Empire can't be very happy that this list has gone missing.

CONFIDENTIAL
Memo 234-AY-4523

Updated Alert: REBEL ACTIVITY, OUTER RIM

The following are considered armed and dangerous enemies of the Empire. If encountered, capture with extreme prejudice:

Name: Unknown
Species: Human
Activity: Leader of rebel fighter ship, modified CEC VCX-100 light freighter. Has engaged in battle with several Imperial craft. Believed to be stealing from Empire and actively seeking to disrupt operations. ARMED, DANGEROUS, AND HIGHLY SOUGHT AFTER.

Name: Unknown
Species: Twi'lek
Activity: Pilot of rebel fighter ship (see above). Highly skilled pilot and tactician. Has evaded major harm or loss, despite inferior craft. Battles have cost the Empire many TIE fighters. ARMED, DANGEROUS, AND HIGHLY SOUGHT AFTER.

WHO ARE THESE GUYS?

Check out my stash
from that TIE!

Got a transceiver calibration plug,
a diagnostic uplink port switch (at
least I think that's what it is), and
oh yeah — a pilot helmet! I've been
wanting one of these types!

It's not the most valuable haul I've ever
pulled in, but I had fun getting it.
Going to lay low for the next few hours
until the Empire finishes
retrieving that pilot and
his wrecked ship.

REBELS RULE

It's funny how a little taste of victory can flip your mood from awful to...not terrible. I'm planning a big score for tomorrow, but tonight I can finally sleep happy.

Okay this is pretty big. Let me start at the beginning, because **WOW.**

My scam today started out okay. I pulled one over on Yogar Lyste (he's the Imperial supply master), got a bunch of electronic leaflets (pretty worthless, but I can strip out their circuitry), a wrench, and a flashlight.

IMPERIAL LOSERS

ELECTRONIC LEAFLETS

FLASHLIGHT

Also got an astromech droid arm. Most people don't know what this crazy thing can do. But in the hands of somebody like me, it's the perfect tool for lock breaking.

It's decent stuff, but the real satisfaction is making Lyste look like an idiot. This grub-chewer is never happy unless he's ruining some merchant's day.

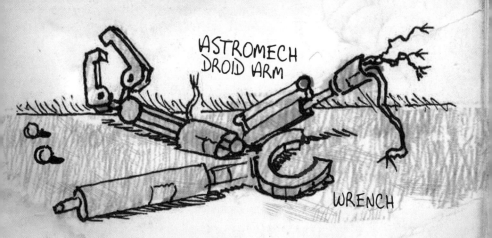

ASTROMECH DROID ARM

WRENCH

TROOPER BLASTER

So then I see these crates. I didn't know it right away, but at least one of these crates was full of blasters. A crate like that is worth a FORTUNE on the black market, and rightfully it was mine.

THAT'S **A LOT** OF BLASTERS!!

I'm not kidding, look at this tech. If I brought these to Ferpil, he'd— Well maybe not Ferpil anymore, but the point is, I could have found somebody to buy them. And I could have been rich.

COOL EXPLOSION

But instead I see a bunch of amateurs trying to muscle in on my score. A girl in armor blowing things up, a big ape, some guy giving orders — they would've brought the whole Empire down on our heads if I hadn't helped them out.

MR TOUGH GUY

REBELS

This is the guy in charge of the
operation: Kanan Jarrus. Who does
he think he is? Trying to steal what
I was going to steal? In my city?

LUCKY I SHOWED UP

Not happy about the way he came in smash-
ing and blasting, when I've spent a ton of time
learning how this city operates. Then he has
the nerve to act like I'm the wild card

This is one of Kanan's battle plans, I borrowed.
Not bad. Could work.

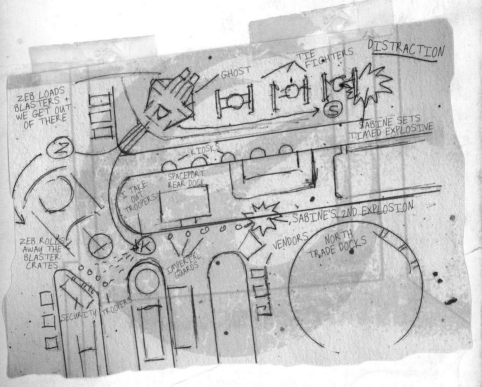

But he looks like a good fighter. And at least
he offered to give me a lift after his crew
botched everything up.

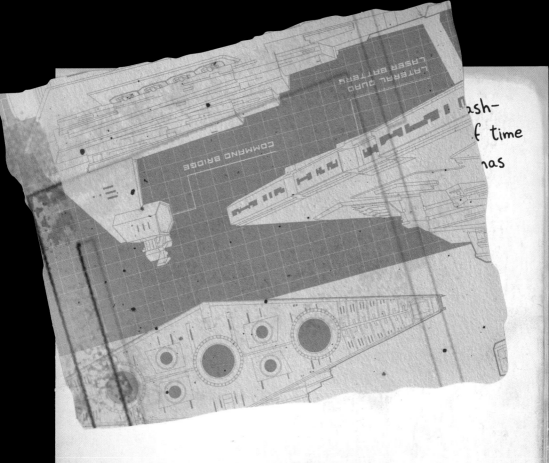

ash-
f time
nas

But he looks like a good fighter. And at least he offered to give me a lift after his crew botched everything up.

And I haven't even gotten to the worst part: this stack of sunshine, Zeb. He's a two-meter tall Lasat and he's a giant jerk.

I agree to come on board their freighter during the escape and he thinks he can lock me in a storeroom? What a nerf herder.

ZEB

His breath stinks too.

According to a crew document I lifted, his real name is "Garazeb Orrelios."

Here are some better names:

Gasbag Old-loser

Zeb the Zero

The Big Stink

Look at this guy

Giant bump on head

long pointy ears

Oversized upper lip

And that smile? What can I say

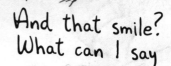

The getaway ship was a space freighter, the Ghost. So we went into space.

THE GHOST

Me. In space. Finally.

It was as amazing as I've always imagined, looking at the stars from the top of the tower.

This ship can scramble its sensor profile — how cool is that? And it's got gun turrets, and a back section that detaches like a starfighter.

SABINE

And then there's Sabine. She was the one in the Mandalorian armor. Seems pretty all right, I guess.

Found this on The Ghost. How to shoot down a TIE fighter!

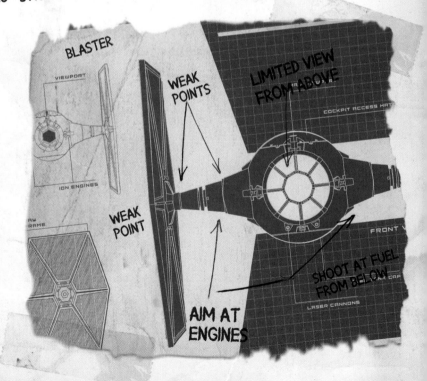

BLASTER

VIEWPORT

ION ENGINES

WEAK POINTS

LIMITED VIEW FROM ABOVE

COCKPIT ACCESS HAT

WEAK POINT

AIM AT ENGINES

SHOOT AT FUEL FROM BELOW

FRONT V

LASER CANNONS

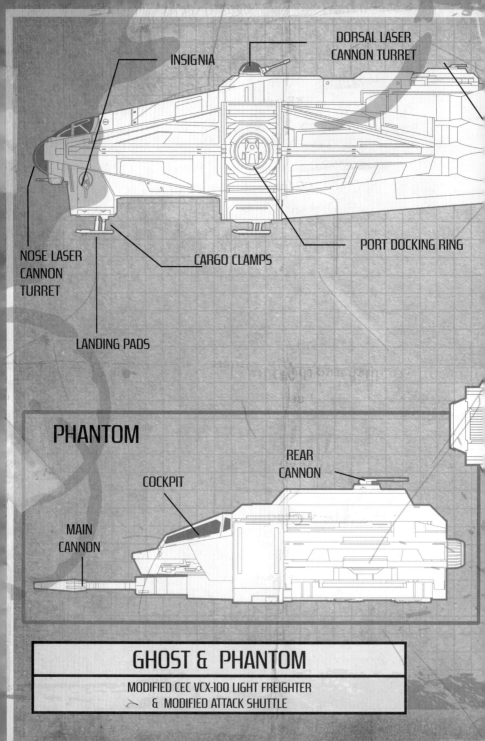

INSIGNIA

DORSAL LASER
CANNON TURRET

NOSE LASER
CANNON
TURRET

CARGO CLAMPS

PORT DOCKING RING

LANDING PADS

PHANTOM

COCKPIT

REAR
CANNON

MAIN
CANNON

GHOST & PHANTOM

MODIFIED CEC VCX-100 LIGHT FREIGHTER
& MODIFIED ATTACK SHUTTLE

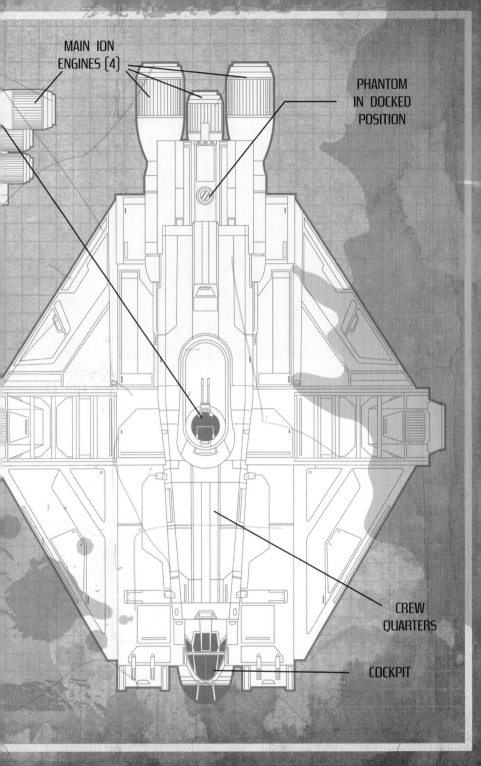

MAIN ION
ENGINES (4)

PHANTOM
IN DOCKED
POSITION

CREW
QUARTERS

COCKPIT

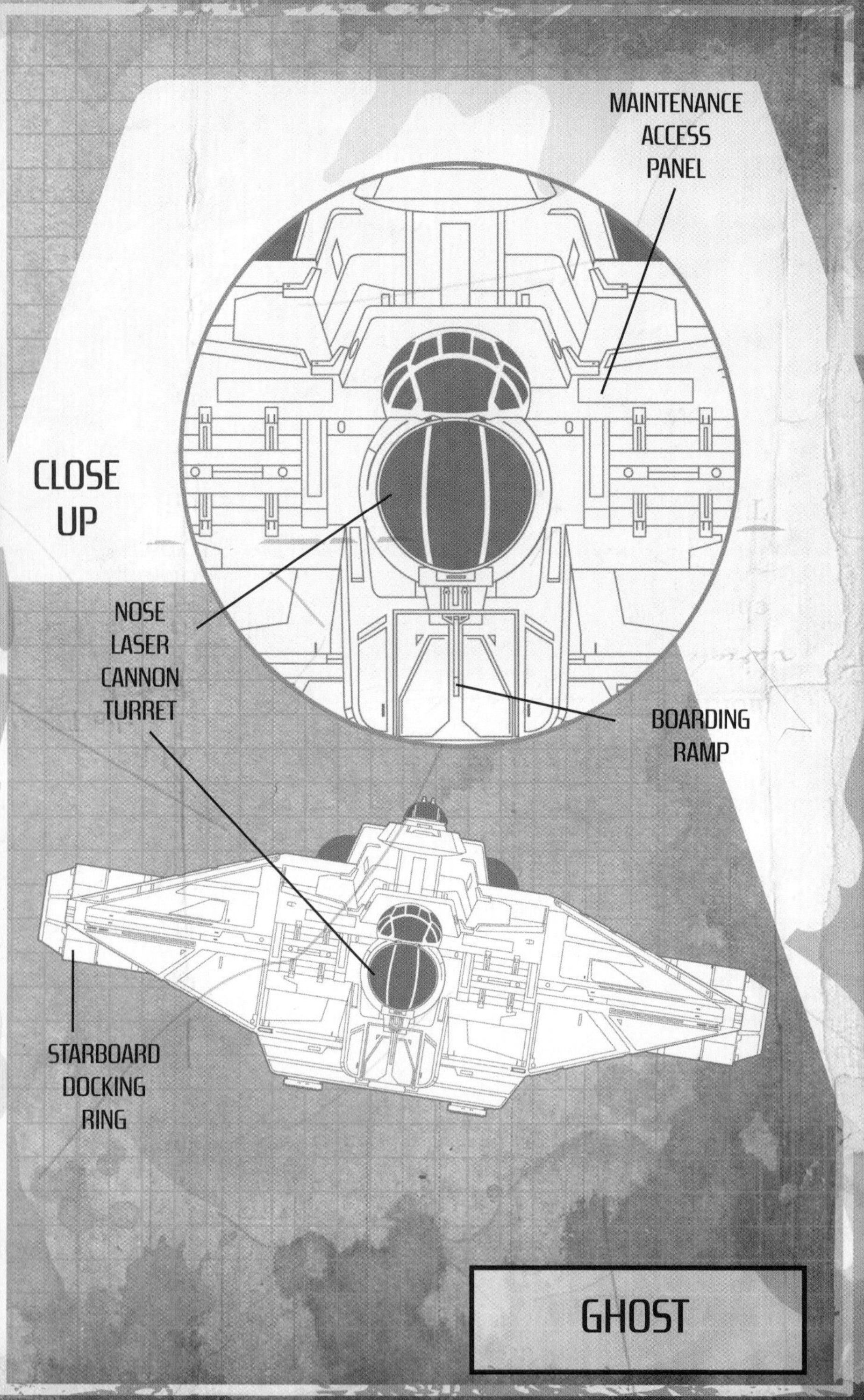

MAINTENANCE
ACCESS
PANEL

CLOSE
UP

NOSE
LASER
CANNON
TURRET

BOARDING
RAMP

STARBOARD
DOCKING
RING

GHOST

Sabine knows a lot about blowing stuff up. And she likes painting, and she doesn't want to talk about her past, which is cool by me. She's a little older than me, but hey, the life I've lived, I'm pretty grown up for my age too.

Here's one of her drawings.

She's pretty good!

Maybe I could show her something I know a lot about? Something not weird?

~~Lothal?~~

~~Helmet collection?~~

~~Slingshot stuff?~~

My drawings?

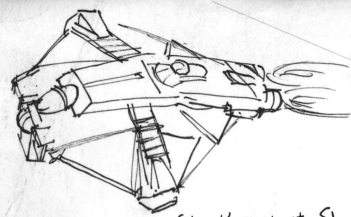

I met Hera in the Ghost's cockpit. She's the one who keeps it flying. Those TIEs chasing us into orbit didn't stand a chance.

I've gotta learn how to pilot a ship. It can't be that much harder than driving my jumpspeeder. Right?

HERA

Even though she was busy she was the only one who seemed to care if I was there or not. Hera looks like she's the one who really keeps this crew together. Because it sure isn't Zeb.

And then there's that droid Chopper or something?

It's got lots of attitude for a machine.

Well, they flew back to Lothal to sell the stolen blasters. My stolen blasters.

We landed in the middle of nowhere, a spot called Tarkintown. I didn't even know this place existed.

It's a sad little slum named for the Imperial governor who kicked everybody out of their homes in Tangletown, and other outlying farming communities. Typical. Those in power don't ask, they just take.

Greetings from Beautiful

TANGLETOWN

Visit our Historic Downtown
Relaxation Oasis of the Outer Rim

FOOD BASKET OF LOTHAL!
— LAND OF FRUIT, SPICE, AND FLAVOR —

I got hungry sometimes, out on my own in the tower. But I had no idea it got this bad. The Ghost crew brought the locals some food. I helped hand it out. Most of the time they have to hunt and scavenge. They cook their meals over tiny grease fires.

The Empire is slowly killing these people. And I think it's only going to get worse.

Anyway, Tarkintown started bringing me down. Nobody was really watching the Ghost, so I figured, why not have a look around? Consider it payback for Zeb shoving me in a closet earlier.

Not sure why, but something drew me to Kanan's quarters. The door was locked—but that's why it's a good thing to have an astromech arm in my pack. All I had to do was plug the scomp link part into the electronic lock, let the arm do its thing, and then—I was in!

There wasn't all that much in Kanan's quarters, so I thought to myself: hidden stash?

Hidden stash! Behind a panel I found this fancy etched holocube-thing. I couldn't get it to work so I figured I'd snatch it and figure it out later.

And there was one other thing—a metal cylinder, like this one. Recognize it? I do, from those holo-stories about Jedi Knights they still sell in the underground markets.

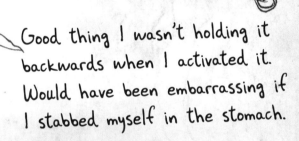

Good thing I wasn't holding it backwards when I activated it. Would have been embarrassing if I stabbed myself in the stomach.

Hey, they should start selling holo-stories about me!

LIBERATION OF LOTHAL:

THE RISE OF EZRA

Kanan caught me with the lightsaber. So I left the lightsaber behind in Kanan's quarters, but I took the cube. Meanwhile the crew of the Ghost sold the stolen blasters to Vizago. Remember him? Big-headed honcho of the Broken Horn syndicate? And in exchange he gave them the flight plan for an Imperial transport supposedly hauling Wookiee slaves.

And these suckers acted all happy about that trade, because it meant they could stage a rescue of those Wookiee prisoners! Like I needed more reminders of why these guys are completely crazy!

REBELS ARE CRAZY

Listen, I'm an expert at sticking it to the Empire. But raiding an armed Imperial transport? Why not just wrap yourself in ribbon and knock on Emperor Palpatine's front door?

IMPERIAL TRANSPORT

Not to mention—they're okay trusting Vizago? Because I've learned to be extra careful around people whose teeth are that sharp.

Anyway, it didn't matter what I had to say.
The Ghost intercepted the transport.

At least they didn't go in guns blazing. Instead they docked, and they tried to pass off Zeb as "a rare HAIRLESS WOOKIEE." That part was hilarious.

The next part—well, I could tell right away something had gone wrong.

They told me to stay on the ship with Hera while the rest of them went deeper into the transport to free the Wookiees. That was fine by me. I didn't need any more reasons to get my head blown off.

But when that shivery chill hit me in my gut...It wasn't the first time I'd felt it, but it was never this bad before.

I tried to warn Hera, but she'd already figured it out. We had walked into a trap.

You see what happens when you trust a crooked crud like Vizago?

In about a microsecond,
      all my worst fears came true.

Imperial Star Destroyers fly over Capital
City all the time, probably just to scare us.
You know what? It works. They're armored
battleships that look like the tips of spears.
They're covered with laser cannons and they're
so HUGE I bet the city's entire population
could fit in one of their kitchens. Star
Destroyers are bigger than pretty much any other
ship in the galaxy. To tell you the truth, I'd
always really wanted to see one up close.

DESTROYER

How many TIEs do they carry on a
    ship this big? A thousand?

So when I looked at the Ghost's sensor board and saw a Star Destroyer closing fast, I wanted to shout, "THAT'S NOT WHAT I MEANT!"

They're always on posters, like this. They're a lot scarier in person.

JOIN THE FLEET

SEE THE GALAXY!

The Star Destroyer was part of the Empire's trap. Even if we managed to escape from the transport, it would blast us before we could reach hyperspace. As it got closer and closer, I knew this was going to be a really, really bad day.

I don't know why I did what I did.

Did Hera make the decision, or did I? We didn't have a lot of time, but she said some words to me that really knocked the fuzz out of my head:

"If all you do is fight for your own life, your life's worth nothing."

And that hurt. And for a second it made me really mad. But in the next second I understood why it made me mad—because it was true.

I don't know what switched inside me, and I don't even know if I could do it again. But the cold feeling in my gut was gone.

I had to do something! Sabine, Kanan, Zeb, Hera—none of them were going to survive if I didn't get moving. So I got moving!

Heck, somebody had to pull their butts out of the garbage masher! Why not me?

I got to Kanan and Zeb just in time. They'd rigged the brig doors to open, but they didn't know that a whole mess of stormtroopers were waiting inside to jump them.

But I activated my slingshot, hit a bulls-eye right square on the detonator packet, and BLAMMO! The first wave of bucketheads fell backwards, and we started running back to the Ghost under the cover of smoke. Those two guys were really lucky I showed up, that's all I can say.

The troopers started getting closer and that's when Sabine did her bit. She'd been hanging out in the transport's gravity control station, and when she and Chopper cut the power everybody suddenly started floating.

But, I should have known better
than to expect a happy ending.

This guy? This is Agent Kallus of
the Imperial Security Bureau. They
don't come much worse than this, but
don't worry, I can take him.

AGENT
LOSER

He got the drop on me, but I would have won
eventually. That is, if Zeb hadn't totally bailed

TIE FIGHTER MO...

ION ENGINES

**AFT LASER TURRET
(DORSAL)**

GRAVITY CONTROL STATION: Because there's always a backup generator for gravity systems, you need two people to take out both units at the same time.

**CORRIDOR WITH
SEALABLE BLAST DOORS**

SIDE VIEW WITH
SHIPS MOUNTED

NTS (ON UNDERSIDE)

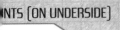

TOP VIEW

POWER COUPLING STATION

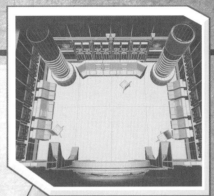

Brig: Supposed to be full of
Wookiees but full of troopers
instead. Not a happy surprise.

Here's where the
Ghost was docked

TOP VIEW
DIAGRAM

TIE FIGHTERS IN
DOCKING POSITION

IMPERIAL FREIGHTER
63.76 M LONG, 31.96 M WIDE

MAIN SENSOR DISH

AFT LASER TURRET
(VENTRAL)

SIDE VIEW (RIGHT SIDE)

BRIDGE

SIDE VIEW (LEFT SIDE)

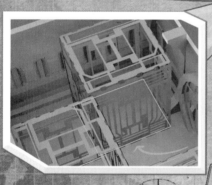

CELL BLOCK
INTERIOR

REINFORCED HWI

FRONT VIEW
DIAGRAM

THANKS ZEB

You heard me. Zeb ditched me. He saw me struggling with Kallus and he must have figured, hey, as long as that big-shot Imperial is busy, let's make our getaway! Without Ezra!

It's like I've always said, you can only count on yourself.

Kallus threw me in the Star Destroyer's brig. He wanted to use me as bait, but I told him good luck with that. Those guys? They're not coming back.

The ISB are the nastiest Imperials around. How nasty? Even other Imperials are scared of them, because they'll arrest anybody who doesn't kiss the Emperor's slippers.

If you're wondering how I got out of the brig, you obviously haven't been keeping notes. It's like I've been saying since the beginning— all you need is a little Ezra magic.

- Use some misdirection. I started coughing like crazy, hoping the guards would check on me and not notice what I was really trying to do.

- Give them something else to worry about. Would you believe Emperor Palpatine is my uncle? The guards didn't either, but it was enough to make them open my cell anyway, just to see that I wasn't dying.

EZRA BRIDGER

- Disappear. I wedged myself up into a corner of the ceiling. Before the guards even thought about looking up, I was out the door.

- Up and over. As soon as I got my stuff back, I went straight into the air shafts.

While listening to the Empire's transmissions, I heard something mind-blowing—the Ghost had returned! The thought that I'd ever see those guys again? Well, it seemed about as unlikely as a pink bantha teleporting into my pocket, but...they had actually come back. For me.

And then that stink-bag Zeb slugged me!

Okay, I was wearing a trooper helmet at the time. But still!

We got away cleanly, thanks to Sabine. She doesn't just create EPIC, DEVASTATING explosions, she makes them look pretty too.

And because I'd kept my ears open while I was on that Star Destroyer, I was able to tell the others where those Wookiees they'd tried to save were now. It wasn't good. The Empire had shipped all the Wookiee slaves off to the spice mines of Kessel.

SLAVERY

I might not know much about Kessel, but I do know that a slave camp is no place for a Wookiee. Or for anybody.

And so that's when I said to the rest of these guys: hey, we started this job. Why not finish it?

This is Spice Mine K-77.

They've been selling all kinds of illegal spice in the black markets of Capital City since forever, but until now I never knew where it came from. Now I hate it even more.

I rescued a Wookiee. Me, Ezra!

He's a cute little guy named Kitwarr, and I brought him back safely to his dad. If that dad ever has another kid he'd better name the next one Ezra, that's all I'm saying.

Just look at these mugshots.

But I didn't tell you how it all happened! So the Ghost flew to Kessel, and we raided the spice mine to free the Wookiees. And I mean we really raided it. The Empire didn't know what to do when we showed up.

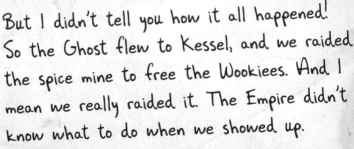

I got to fight side by side with Kanan, who busted out that lightsaber I let him keep. And like I said before, I rescued a Wookiee. I'm pretty proud of that. Even if I'm still picking fur off of my clothes.

Is this what it's like to be a hero? I could get used to it.

And it turns out that Sabine understands a little Wookiee. Listening to her translate, I found out that the Wookiees had started calling me "the little warrior." Awesome!

But then I started thinking...

JEDI

I kept coming back to that stuff I'd found in Kanan's quarters: the cube and the lightsaber. I kind of skipped over this, but when I was held prisoner aboard the Star Destroyer I accidentally got that cube working.

It isn't just a fancy-looking relic. It's a Jedi Holocron. It acted like it sensed my thoughts somehow. It sort of unfolded while I stared at it, then it played a recording for me. And now the questions won't stop.

THE FORCE

MASTER

Who is this Obi-Wan Kenobi I saw in the hologram? What was his message all about?

What did he mean by "Trust in the Force"?

What's the deal with the Jedi, anyway? I thought Emperor Palpatine wiped them all out. And now the guy in the message tells me the Emperor is actually a Sith Lord? Could this whole thing get any crazier?

What does all of this mean?

One thing's for sure:
I'm not going to figure
it out on my own.

I've made a decision—
I'm going to join the crew of
the Ghost.
They need a guy like me.

I'll miss my old comm tower, but I'm definitely
not going to miss that leak in the roof.

Bunking with Zeb won't be too bad, as
long as the ratty muscle-head remembers
to take a bath once in a while. And I
guess I'll let Kanan show me what he
knows about the Force, or whatever it is
those guys do.

EZRA THE
HERO?

This is crewman Ezra Bridger, signing off for now. I still can't believe I've written all this down, but it's been kinda fun. Perhaps some Lothal kid will discover this book someday and even read it. If you do, well, I hope you learned something. Then make a fortune selling this.

Selfie

And, oh yeah—Trust in the Force.

Transport ship

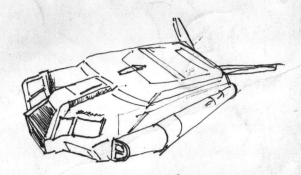

Saw these in the spaceport
docking station 6

FIGHT THE EMPIRE

REBELS RULE

Writer: Daniel Wallace
Editor: Neil Wertheimer
Art Director, Designer, and Illustrator: Andrew Barthelmes
Page Layout: Gretchen Schuler-Dandridge
Copy Editor: Jay Gissen
Managing Editor: Christine Guido
Creative Director: Julia Sabbagh
Associate Publisher: Rosanne McManus
Lucasfilm Editor: Joanne Chan
Lucasfilm Story Group: Leland Chee, Pablo Hidalgo